ABOUT THE BOOK

Sam loves to play soccer. He loves
to hit the ball with his foot and with
his knee. But with his head? Not Sam!
That's why the other team members
call him "Soft Skull Sam." One day
a visitor shows the players all sorts of
soccer tricks, including how to make
successful head shots. But Sam still
ducks when he sees the ball coming.

Then, in the middle of an exciting
match, Sam tries one of the new tricks
with unexpected results! The surprise
ending will delight readers and make
this another favorite by the much-loved
author and artist, Syd Hoff.

Soft Skull

HARCOURT BRACE JOVANOVICH   NEW YORK AND LONDON

Sam

Written and illustrated by Syd Hoff

(HBJ)

Copyright © 1981 by Syd Hoff
All rights reserved. No part of this publication may be reproduced or
transmitted in any form or by any means, electronic or mechanical,
including photocopy, recording, or any information storage and
retrieval system, without permission in writing from the publisher.

Requests for permission to make copies of any part of the work
should be mailed to: Permissions, Harcourt Brace Jovanovich, Inc.,
757 Third Avenue, New York. New York 10017.

Printed in the United States of America

LIBRARY OF CONGRESS CATALOGING IN PUBLICATION DATA
Hoff, Sydney.
Soft Skull Sam.
(A Let me read book)
SUMMARY: Sam loves everything about soccer but the all-
important head shot.
[1. Soccer—Fiction] I. Title.
PZ7.H672So   [Fic]   80-24590
ISBN 0-15-277062-3   ISBN 0-15-277063-1 (pbk.)

B C D E   FIRST EDITION   B C D E (PBK.)

Sam loved soccer.
He was proud to be on a team.

He loved to hit the ball
with his foot.

He loved to hit the ball
with his knee.

The only thing Sam didn't like was
to hit the ball with his *head*.
When he saw a "header" coming
toward him, Sam always ducked.

"Soft Skull Sam" his teammates
called him.

One day Sam had an idea.
He went home and got his
father's hard hat and put it
on his head. "Now they can
drop a rock on me," said Sam.

"Where do you think you're going
with my hard hat?" his father asked.
"I'm going to play soccer," said Sam.
"No, you're not. I need that hat
on my job," said his father.

The next day Sam went back
to the soccer field.
"I'll go on playing no matter
what they call me," he said.

"You can't be a soccer player
if you're afraid of the ball,"
said Marjorie Ann, who was on
his team. "Come on, I'll throw it easy."

She threw the ball to Sam.
He ducked just in time.

The ball hit Mr. Fleming,
the coach, instead.

"Hey!" said Mr. Fleming. "I've had
enough of this, Sam. I'm going
to call the doctor."

The doctor turned out to be
"Doc" Stengel, who had been a
soccer star in college.

"The human skull is very hard,"
he explained. "A header doesn't
hurt if you learn to hit it right."

He showed Sam different ways to hit the ball with his head. "I will show you some other tricks too," said Doc.

He showed him how to trap a
ball with his chest or thigh.

He showed him how to twist his
body when he dribbled a ball.

Then he showed Sam how to kick.
"The trick is to kick with your
instep, rather than your toes. Then
the ball will go straight," he said.
"But the best shot is a head shot."

Sam threw the ball, and the doctor
bounced it off his head into the net.

That week, Sam practiced all the
tricks Doc Stengel had shown him.
But he still couldn't help
ducking every head shot.

Then Sam's team played its next
game. It was a close one. In the
second half, Marjorie Ann dribbled
the ball up the field.

The other team tried to take
the ball away from her.
She kicked the ball to Sam.

It was a high ball.
Sam ran forward, hoping he
could trap it with his chest.

Instead the ball hit Sam on the head
and went into the net for a goal!

"Hooray for Sam!" his teammates
shouted, and they slapped him on the back.
Sam looked surprised.
"It didn't hurt at all," he said.

Before the game was over, Sam made
three more headers. When his team
won, his teammates carried him off
the field on their shoulders.

"Sam is one guy who
knows how to use his head
in this game!" they said.
And everyone cheered.

SYD HOFF has written and illustrated
countless picture books for children.
He is known internationally for
his cartoons; the first was sold to
The New Yorker when he was only
seventeen. Mr. Hoff was born in
New York City and attended
the National Academy of Design.
He and his wife live in Florida.